Splish, Splash, Splosh!

T0337179

Written by Tom Ottway

Illustrated by Anna Kazimi

Collins

What's in this story?

Listen and say

eggs

puddle

sand

paint

water

Jade and Jack are cooking.

In the kitchen ... with some eggs!

Now Jack and Jade are painting.

Now Jack and Jade are jumping in the puddles.

Jade and Jack are playing in the sand.

In the sand ... jumping, jumping!

They are very dirty now!

In the garden with the water ...

UH-OH! Jade and Jack's boots are very dirty!

Let's clean our boots now!

Splish, splash, splosh!

UH-OH! Jack and Jade's hands are very dirty!

They are cleaning their hands now.

UH-OH! The kitchen is very dirty!

With the water. Clean it, clean it!

Now the kitchen is clean again!

Picture dictionary

Listen and repeat

clean

dirty

garden

kitchen

cook

jump

paint

After reading

1 Look and order the story

2 Listen and say

Collins

Published by Collins
An imprint of HarperCollins*Publishers*
Westerhill Road
Bishopbriggs
Glasgow
G64 2QT

HarperCollins*Publishers*
1st Floor, Watermarque Building
Ringsend Road
Dublin 4
Ireland

William Collins' dream of knowledge for all began with the publication of his first book in 1819.

A self-educated mill worker, he not only enriched millions of lives, but also founded a flourishing publishing house. Today, staying true to this spirit, Collins books are packed with inspiration, innovation and practical expertise. They place you at the centre of a world of possibility and give you exactly what you need to explore it.

© HarperCollins*Publishers* Limited 2020

10 9 8 7 6 5 4 3 2

ISBN 978-0-00-839771-5

Collins® and COBUILD® are registered trademarks of HarperCollins*Publishers* Limited

www.collins.co.uk/elt

British Library Cataloguing in Publication Data

A catalogue record for this publication is available from the British Library.

Author: Tom Ottway
Illustrator: Anna Kazimi (Beehive)
Series editor: Rebecca Adlard
Publishing manager: Lisa Todd
Product managers: Jennifer Hall and Caroline Green
In-house editor: Alma Puts Keren
Project manager: Emily Hooton
Editor: Deborah Friedland
Proofreaders: Natalie Murray and Michael Lamb
Cover designer: Kevin Robbins
Typesetter: 2Hoots Publishing Services Ltd
Audio produced by id audio, London
Reading guide author: Emma Wilkinson
Production controller: Rachel Weaver
Printed and bound by: GPS Group, Slovenia

MIX
Paper from
responsible sources

FSC
www.fsc.org

FSC™ C007454

Download the audio for this book and a reading guide for parents and teachers at www.collins.co.uk/839771